The Flop-Eared Hound

by Ellis Credle

Illustrations by *ArtStudio Earth22* based on original photography by Charles Townsend

Cover design by Tina DeKam

Cover illustration by Nada Serafimovic

Originally published in 1938

This unabridged version has updated grammar and spelling.

© 2019 Jenny Phillips

www.goodandbeautiful.com

To Aunt Mary

and the kindly folk

on her plantation

A way down South in a little cabin underneath a honey-pod tree, there lived a little boy named Shadrack Meshack Abednego Jones.

Nobody ever called Shadrack Meshack Abednego Jones by his real name except on Sundays and very special occasions. It was much too long and hard to say. They just called him little Boot-jack.

One morning while his mammy was washing clothes, little Boot-jack sat beside her with his head in his hands.

"Little Boot-jack, why don't you go play?" asked his mammy.

"Haven't got anybody to play with," said little Boot-jack, and he sat and sat.

"I'm so lonesome," said little Boot-jack. "Haven't got any brothers, haven't got any sisters, haven't got anybody to play with, and I'm so lonesome!"

Just then, away down in the barn lot, he heard something go, "Ow-o-o-o-o! Ow-o-o-o-o!"

"What's that?" asked little Boot-jack, and he jumped up and ran to find out what the noise was.

"Ow-o-o-o!" came the sound again. Boot-jack looked all around, and after a while, he spied a flop-eared hound.

"Hey-o there, you old flop-eared hound!" little Boot-jack greeted him.

"Ow-o-o-o!" said the flop-eared hound lonesomely.

"What's the matter with you, old flop-eared hound?" asked little Boot-jack.

"Ow-o-o-o!" howled the hound.

"I reckon you are hungry," said little Boot-jack. He went into the house and brought out a plate full of hoecake. The hound ate it all, all up.

"Are you all right now?" asked little Boot-jack.

"Ow-o-o-o!" said the hound as lonesomely as before.

"Maybe you are thirsty," said little Boot-jack, and he took the flop-eared hound to the well and gave him a drink.

"Now I reckon you are all right," said Boot-jack.

But the hound said, "Ow-o-o-o-o-o-o-o!"

"What's the matter with you, flop-eared hound?" asked little Boot-jack. "You've had something to eat. You've had something to drink, and you are still howling as though you had lost your last friend."

Little Boot-jack led the hound to his mammy, and he said, "Mammy, what's the matter with this old hound? He's had something to eat. He's had something to drink, and he's still howling."

"Reckon that old hound hasn't got any home," said Mammy, "and everything living is lonesome if he hasn't any home."

"Let me keep this old lonesome hound, Mammy," begged little Boot-jack. "Then I'll have somebody to play with."

"Ask your pappy," replied Mammy. "If he says all right, then you can keep him."

Down the field path went little Boot-jack. Pappy was busy plowing peanuts.

"Look-a-here, Pappy," called Boot-jack, "may I keep this old flop-eared hound? He's come to our house 'cause he hasn't got any home."

"Whoa, mule!" cried Pappy. He stopped

plowing and looked at the hound. "You can keep him," said he, "provided he will behave himself and act as he ought to."

"Thanky, sir!" cried little Boot-jack.

And the hound's tail went thump, thump, thump.

"I'll tell you what we'll do," said Boot-jack to the flop-eared hound. "Let's go down to the creek and catch a little fish for dinner."

"Wuff, wuff!" agreed the hound.

Boot-jack got his fishing pole and dug

some worms, and away they went, along

beside the sunflower patch, over the fields,

through the woods, and after a while, they
came to the creek.

Along the edge of the creek, they saw
a little baby turtle. The flop-eared hound
jumped at him.

"Wuff, wuff!" he barked. But the baby
turtle was too quick for him. He jerked in
his head, pulled in his tail and all four feet,
and there was nothing left but his hard little
house.

"Aren't you ashamed, you great big old
dog, trying to scare that little turtle out
of his wits!" cried little Boot-jack. And he
picked up the baby turtle, house and all,
and put him safely into the water. The little
turtle stretched out his head, paddled with
his feet, and went swimming away as fast as
he could go.

Boot-jack sat upon the bank and threw his line into the water. Pretty soon he felt something pulling. He gave a jerk, and up came a nice little fish!

"Wuff, wuff!" barked the flop-eared hound. He jumped for the fish and got himself all tangled up in the fishing line.

Ker-splash! Over he fell into the water, and he jerked little Boot-jack right in after him.

"Ugh! Ugh!" spluttered Boot-jack as he came up out of the water. "Just look what you've done, you old flop-eared hound! You've made me fall in the water and get my clothes all wet and muddy, and my nice little fish has wriggled off the hook and swum clean away!"

Little Boot-jack was all wet and muddy. He did not dare go home that way. He cleaned the mud all off in front and sat down in the sun a long, long time to let his clothes get dry. At last he went along home, and the hound followed at his heels.

"Gracious sakes, boy—where have you been so long?" asked Mammy. "And what's that all over your back?" She leaned over and looked sharply at little Boot-jack. "Mud

all over your back! Bet you fell into that
creek," she cried.

Boot-jack hung his head. He did not want
to tell on the flop-eared hound.

"That old dog is at the bottom of this!"
cried Mammy. "I'll bet on that. He's going to
be a troublemaker. Maybe you'd better carry
him off right now, before he makes more
mischief."

"He's not going to make any more mischief, Mammy," cried Boot-jack. "He's going to be just like an angel all the time."

"Well, he'd better be," declared Mammy,

"because if he makes any more trouble, he'll have to go away from here."

The next day, nobody said anything about taking the hound away. Along about ten o'clock, Mammy brought out a tin bucket and said to little Boot-jack, "Take this bucket and go out to the orchard and pick us some apples. We're going to have some apple dumplings for dinner."

Little Boot-jack smiled a broad smile. He took the bucket, and away he went. The flop-eared hound went trotting along behind.

As they were passing through a little stretch of woods, Boot-jack heard a rustling in the bushes. He looked, and there, sitting on top of a big round stump, was a little baby possum. The flop-eared hound dashed after him.

"Wuff, wuff!" he barked fiercely. The possum took one look and fell over on his side. There he lay as though he were dead.

"Now look what you've done, you old flop-eared hound!" cried little Boot-jack. "You've scared that little possum clean to death!"

But the possum was only pretending, "playing possum." As soon as Boot-jack and his dog were out of sight, he got up again and climbed way, way up a great big oak tree.

Boot-jack picked apples until his bucket was full to the top, and then he went home again.

"Uh-huh!" said Mammy when she saw the bucket full of shining apples. "We're going to have some of the best apple dumplings you ever stuck your teeth into!"

She got to work and made four beautiful apple dumplings and put them on the fire to cook. When they were all nicely brown, she took them out and set them to cool on the table in the front room.

Pretty soon the flop-eared hound began to smell those dumplings. He put his paws

on the table and took one taste. Then—he ate up one apple dumpling. He ate up two apple dumplings. He ate up three apple dumplings. He ate up four apple dumplings! And that was all there was!

When Mammy came back into the room, she found the platter licked as clean as if it had been washed.

"Gracious me!" she cried. "What has happened to my nice apple dumplings?" She turned and frowned at little Boot-jack. "Shadrack Meshack Abednego Jones, did you eat up my dumplings?"

"No, ma'am!" replied Boot-jack. "Honest to goodness, I haven't even been in the room!"

Mammy's eye fell on the flop-eared hound. His mouth was all smeared with apple juice. "Here's the one that ate up all those dumplings!" she cried. "You, Boot-jack,

take this old dog and carry him off and give him away!"

Little Boot-jack tied a rope around the hound's neck and led him slowly down the road. Along and along he went, and after a while, he came to a great white house.

"Hello there, little Boot-jack!"

Boot-jack looked, and there, trotting around the corner of the house, was a lady on horseback. It was Miss Mary, who owned the big white house and the little cabin where Boot-jack lived and all the land around about.

"Where are you going with that flop-eared hound?" asked Mary.

"Just looking for a home for this old hound," replied Boot-jack. "Maybe you'd like to have him?"

"Well, I think I would," said Miss Mary. "We like dogs at this house, and there's always room for one more."

Little Boot-jack handed her the dog's rope and went home all alone.

Little Boot-jack sat on the cabin steps with his head in his hands.

"What's the matter with you, little Boot-jack?" asked Mammy.

"I feel so lonesome for my old flop-eared hound," replied little Boot-jack.

"Well, the very best cure for lonesomeness is hard work," said Mammy. "I'm going to send you out to help Pappy in the peanut field."

All afternoon Boot-jack drove a mule up and down between the rows of peanut plants. His pappy pulled up the clumpy peanut plants, shook off the dirt, and

loaded them into the cart. When it was full, Boot-jack drove the cart to the barn.

His mammy hung the peanut plants in the barn to dry.

All the while, Boot-jack kept thinking of

the flop-eared hound. "Reckon my dog is gone for good," he said sadly.

But the next morning, as Boot-jack was feeding the pigs, there was a great noise in the bushes.

Away ran the little pigs, snorting, "Ooof, oof, oof!"

"Who's that?" cried little Boot-jack. "Who's that in the bushes, scaring the little pigs away from their breakfast?"

Cra-a-a-sh! went something in the bushes, and who should come bounding through but the flop-eared hound!

"Well, if it isn't my old dog!" cried Boot-jack joyfully, and he hugged the flop-eared hound so tightly that his ribs creaked.

"I tell you what we'll do. Let's go to the persimmon tree and get a taste of persimmons."

"Wuff, wuff!" barked the hound joyfully, and off they went through the cornfield and along toward the pasture where the persimmon tree was.

After a while they came to the persimmon tree. But it was too high to climb.

"I'll go get a ladder," said little Boot-jack. And he did. Up the ladder he went, and he tasted the persimmons. But the persimmons were so green that they drew Boot-jack's

mouth up into a knot. "Ooof!" he cried.
"Can't eat these green 'simmons. Get out of
my way, flop-eared hound; I'm coming down
this tree."

"Wuff, wuff!" barked the flop-eared
hound. He bounded out of the way,
bumped into the ladder, and down it came,
bum-a-lum-lum!

"Look what you've done, you old
flop-eared hound!" cried little Boot-jack.
"Now I can't get down from this high tree!"

Boot-jack sat and sat and sat all morning.
After a while dinner time came, and he
could hear his Mammy calling.

"Boot-jack, oh, BOOT-JA-A-A-CK!"

"Here I am, Mammy!" cried Boot-jack as
loud as he could holler. But he could not
make his Mammy hear him, and it was a

long time before Pappy came looking for him and took him down from the tree.

Mammy was all out of humor because little Boot-jack had not come home for his dinner. "Where did that old dog come from?" she cried. "Didn't you take him off and give him away as I told you to do?"

"Yes, ma'am, but he came back," said Boot-jack.

"Well, he's just a troublemaker," said Mammy. "Tie a rope around his neck and carry him so far that he won't ever come back!"

Boot-jack tied a rope on the hound's neck and led him sadly down the road.

After a while he came to a tall barn. His Uncle Andy was there, sitting on a chair by the wall, reading his Bible.

"Hey there, little Boot-jack," called Uncle

Andy. "Where are you going with that flop-eared hound?"

"Just taking him off to lose him," replied Boot-jack.

"Does he know how to hunt possums?" asked Uncle Andy.

"Reckon he does," said Boot-jack. "He's a mighty smart dog."

"Well, you can lose him right here with me!" said Uncle Andy. "There isn't anything I like better than possum hunting."

Little Boot-jack gave him the dog and started along home feeling very sad.

"Ow-o-o-o!" howled the flop-eared hound lonesomely.

When he got home, his Mammy said,

"Don't you think anymore about that no-count hound. You come into the house. I'm going to cook some nice batter cakes for your supper."

Boot-jack followed his mammy into the

neat little kitchen at the back of the house. Mammy mixed a big batch of batter cakes and cooked them over the fire.

Boot-jack ate plenty of batter cakes, but they did not make him forget the flop-eared hound. After he went to bed, he dreamed that his dog had come back.

The next morning, when he went out on

the back porch to wash his face, who should
be waiting there but the flop-eared hound.

"Gracious me! Here's my old dog again!"
cried little Boot-jack. "Reckon he got
lonesome for me, just as I did for him!"

That day, while Mammy and Pappy and
little Boot-jack were in the field picking cotton,
the flop-eared hound got into the house.

He found Pappy's Sunday go-to-meeting shoes and chewed them all to pieces.

That put Pappy in a very bad humor with the flop-eared hound. "This time," he said, "I'm going to take that old dog away myself. I'm going to take him so far that he won't *ever* come back!"

That very afternoon, he hitched up the old

mule and set out for town. The flop-eared hound sat mournfully in the foot of the buggy.

When Pappy came back, the flop-eared hound was not with him, and little Boot-jack felt very sad.

"Never mind about that no-count hound," said Pappy. "There's a big circus in the town tomorrow, and I'm going to take you. You'll see more sights than you ever saw in your life before!"

The next day, little Boot-jack put on his tan-colored trousers and his blouse with a blue collar, and off they started for the circus. When they came to the town, he looked this way and that. "Wish I could see my old dog," said he. But the flop-eared hound was nowhere to be seen.

Boot-jack had never seen anything like that circus. There were elephants and monkeys and tigers and giraffes and a funny old clown with a great big nose. He came over to the place where they sat and shook hands with little Boot-jack.

After it was all over, they set out for home. Mammy filled the buggy with so many bundles that little Boot-jack had to stand on the back. Away went the mule, lickety-split, through the town and out on the country road. Boot-jack hung on for dear life, but the buggy went over a big bump, and—ker-thump! He bounced right off!

Mammy and Pappy went rolling along and left little Boot-jack sitting in the middle of the road.

"Wait! Wait!" shouted Boot-jack. He

jumped up and ran after them. But the buggy went rattle-bang, and nobody heard him calling.

When Mammy and Pappy got home, they looked around for little Boot-jack.

"Oh, oh, oh!" cried Mammy. "What has happened to Boot-jack?"

"Reckon he fell off somewhere," said Pappy.

They turned the buggy around and drove back, looking on this side and that side. But little Boot-jack was nowhere to be seen. After a while it began to grow dark.

"Oh, oh, oh!" sobbed Mammy. "What in the world has happened to my child?"

Just then she heard something go "Ow-o-o-o-o! Ow-o-o-o-o!"

"What's that?" asked Mammy.

"Well, if it isn't that old flop-eared hound,"

said Pappy. "Reckon he's trying to find his way back to our house."

"He's got such a good nose, maybe he can find our little boy," said Mammy. "Go find Boot-jack!" she shouted. "Boot-jack is lost! Go find him!"

The flop-eared hound put his nose to the ground. Snuff, snuff, snuff! He went smelling along.

After a while he made off into the bushes.

"Wuff, wuff, *WUFF*!" he barked. "WUFF! WUFF!"

Mammy and Pappy jumped out of the buggy to see what he had found. And there, lying in a pile of leaves, all tear-stained and fast asleep, was little Boot-jack.

"Oh! Here's my child!" cried Mammy. "This old hound found him!" She snatched up

little Boot-jack and hugged him as tight as ever she could.

That night when little Boot-jack went to bed, the flop-eared hound stretched out right beside him.

"Mammy," said Boot-jack sleepily, "are you going to let my dog stay here this time?"

"I certainly am," said Mammy. "He's not ever going to be lonesome anymore because he's got a home for the rest of his life!"

And she kissed little Boot-jack goodnight.

THE END